Something Strange Across the River

First published paperback edition by One Peace Books, Inc. in 2013

Author Kafu Nagai
Translated by Glenn Anderson

Cover Design Shimpachi Inoue

One Peace Books
43-32 22nd Street #204 Long Island City, NY 11101 USA
http://www.onepeacebooks.com

Printed in Canada

Something Strange Across the River

Kafu Nagai
Translated by Glenn Anderson

Chapter One

I had essentially never been to see a motion picture.

It's a vague memory now, but it must have been sometime around 1897. There was a theater in the back of a department store in Kanda. They had filmed the streets and scenes of San Francisco. I think it was around that time that the term "motion picture" first came into use. It's been forty years or so since then, and apparently they don't say "motion picture" anymore, but it's what I grew up with and it rolls off the tongue, so I'll keep on calling them "motion pictures."

After the earthquake a young author came to visit me at my home and quickly picked up on my antiquated speech habits, at which point he told me the world would leave me behind if I didn't make an effort to catch up. He brought me, against my will mind you, to a small theater in Asakusa. It had apparently received excellent reviews at the time. When we sat down to watch it I discovered that it was an adaptation of a Maupassant short story, at which point I lost all interest in the film. Why not simply read the original? It was sure to be superior anyway, I thought, and I made a point of expressing my opinion at the time.

However, I realize that nowadays young and old alike watch motion pictures and apparently enjoy them enough to turn them into an everyday topic of conversation, and if I wanted to have the slightest grasp of their bantering it would not be unwise of me to cultivate the most basic of knowledge regarding them—a disposition of mine which manifests itself the moment I pass a theater on the street. I make a point to stop and read the names of the motion pictures they are exhibiting. A glance at the posters and one can easily imagine the contents and mood of the thing without actually viewing the picture, and it is typically enough to get an idea of what others enjoy about them should they become a topic of conversation.

There is perhaps no better place to steal glances at theater posters than Asakusa Park. A walk around the park and one may glimpse advertisements for all manner of motion pictures, which is an opportunity to decide for oneself the quality of their workmanship. Without fail, whenever I leave the park for Asakusa, I drag the tip of a stick across the surface of the lake and recall the names of the pictures from the posters.

It happened one day, around the time when the evening breezes had begun to grow ever cooler. I'd seen my share of the motion picture posters that sat at the entrances of the excess of shops, and satisfied, left from the far end of the park, heading for Senzoku. Kototoi Bridge was on my right and Iriya sprawled out to the left. I had paused for a moment in consideration of the land and what path I might wish to take through it, when a man of approximately forty appeared at my elbow. He was dressed in a tattered western-styled suit.

"Good sir, feeling lonely? Allow me to introduce

you to someone?"

"No, thank you." I hurried my pace to put distance between us.

He matched my pace and kept at my side. "This is a rare chance, man. Sir. She's wild."

"I'm just fine. I'm on my way to Yoshiwara."

I couldn't tell if he was a pimp or if he just worked for a geisha house, but he appeared untrustworthy to say the least, and as I do not enjoy being wrangled by suspicious strangers I had quickly—and without much thought—declared that I was headed for Yoshiwara. It was an attempt to shake him off, but it served to decide the destination of my previously aimless wandering, and in the course of traveling there I recalled a little secondhand bookshop I liked to patronize. It was hidden in an alleyway off the banks of the river.

There is a large gate that sits where the Iriya River meets up with the underground culverts, and it conceals a darkened backstreet, tucked in its shadows. Buildings lined one side of the street, while on the other side of the embankment the backside of walls, delineating private property, continued in rows visible just over the lip of the embankment. Houses lined the near side, interspersed with the wider storefronts of dealers of pipes and bricks and wood and clays and so forth. The houses grew smaller to fit alongside the narrowing canal. The street was lit only by lanterns dangling from nearby bridges. Once I'd left the canal and bridges behind I discovered that pedestrian traffic had all but disappeared. By that time of night, the only lights to be seen were from the tobacco shop and the secondhand bookshop.

I couldn't recall the name of the store, though the shop distinguished itself by the products they had put up for display. They had copies of *Literary Club* from the time of its founding up with old *Yamato* newspapers (interview supplements attached). Not to say that their interesting finds were not sequestered in heaps of junk. However, I did not go so far out of my way, I didn't make a special trip there, for the *books*, no—I made the trip for the overwhelming sense of humanity effused by both the owner and the little town surrounding the shop.

The owner was an older man with perfectly cropped hair capping his small frame. He was well over sixty from what I could tell. Everything from his face, his demeanor, his language, his kimono, even the way he wore his clothes contained a quintessential element of small-town Tokyo— persisting despite the times, persisting without fear of alteration or degradation—and appeared, to my eyes, more nostalgic and respectable than even the most rare tomes that adorned his shelves. Before the earthquake I would meet one or two of these smart older Edo types anytime I would go to the theater or visit a hall. I'd often see *Tame* or *Kikugoro* or *Ichizo*, who worked for *Sandanji*. I'm sure they have all passed on by now.

When I slid open the glass door of the shop, the owner was sitting, as he always was, near the edge of a paper screen with his rounded back slanting slightly to the outside, his glasses perched at the end of his nose, head buried in reading material. Granted, I was always sure to visit around seven or eight in the evening, but he was always sure to be seated in precisely the same manner: At the sound of the sliding door, without altering the stoop of his back, he would roll his neck slightly in the direction of the entrance and drawl, "Come on in now," before slipping his glasses off, lurching slowly to his feet, patting the dust from his cushion, and smoothing himself down, finally turning and giving a proper greeting. Neither his greeting nor his demeanor varied from the conventional.

"As you can see, not much has changed. Not much that you can see anyway. Well, we did get some old *Hotan* magazines in—not that we have the whole collection though."

"The *Tamenagashi Shunko* magazine?"

"Sure, well, we have the first printing. Care to see it?" Now muttering to himself, "Where did I put that thing?", he pulled five or six books from a stack that was leaning against the wall, brushing the dust from them and politely passing one of them in my direction.

"Says 1879. God, these old things make me feel like a kid again. If you had a full set of the *Roh Literature Report*, I'd love to take it off your hands."

"We get them in here sometimes, but never a full set. They're all over the place."

"You don't happen to have any *Gekka* magazines, do you?"

"Of course."

The glass door rattled open and the owner and I turned to look—another one well over sixty ducked in. He was bald, and his cheeks were sunken deep. He gave off a hint of destitution; perhaps it was the dirty, striped bathrobe he flung onto a stack of old books by the door.

"I hate those automobiles. Those things almost killed me today."

"Well, they're cheap and convenient—or that's what they say anyway. But—hey now, you didn't get hurt or nothing?"

"My amulet broke—I think that's what saved me. There was a big crash, with a bus and a taxi. Get goose bumps just remembering it. Anyway, I went out to the Hatogaya market today and bought the strangest thing—I love these old things, and they don't make 'em like they used to. I don't really know who would buy it, but when I saw it I just couldn't keep myself from picking it up.

Baldy quickly began to undo his package of cloth, and produced from it a simple woman's kimono and a singlet, its sleeves of a different fabric than its body. The kimono was gray and printed with a simple, delicate pattern. The sleeves of the singlet were a bit odd as well. Neither of them appeared very old, I would have dated them near the Restoration. I was struck by the singlet, and realized it would work well for mounting woodblock prints or lining book slipcases, or even covering up Edo picture serials. I asked the bookseller to wrap it up with the old magazines.

I wanted to catch a ride up the riverside so I spent

a little while waiting by the large gate. The incessant shouting of the taxis quickly grew tiresome however, so I soon ducked back into the small, dark alleyway where the trains and taxis didn't run. Skulking off down the street it wasn't long before I caught sight of the lights from Kototoi Bridge in between the towering trees. I had heard the park at the end of the river was boisterous and loud, so instead of heading out to the mouth of the river I followed a little street lined with electric lights to an area where a heavy chain was suspended between posts, and I took a seat on it.

Actually on the way I had stopped to purchase some bread and a can of food, which I had wrapped in a handkerchief. I undid the bundle and tried to wrap the old magazine inside as well but the combination of soft objects and hard objects, as well as their size, proved to complicate the task. Realizing that it would be easiest if I moved the can into my overcoat pocket I spread the handkerchief out on the lawn and was fully invested in shuffling the arrangement of the objects when, without warning, someone stepped from the shadow of a tree behind me and barked, "You there, what do you think you're doing?" I heard the sound of a saber scraping from its sheath. The policeman stepped into view and grabbed me roughly by the shoulder.

I did not immediately answer. Instead I tended to the knot of my parcel, ensuring it was tight and proper, before standing and facing him. He was apparently unable to tolerate the silence and quickly grabbed my elbow, pushing me and growling, "Go over there."

He led me down a small street in the park and out to the lip of Kototoi Bridge, where there was a small police box situated near the main street. He dragged me there before handing me roughly to the officer on duty and storming off, no doubt to fulfill his much more pressing duties.

The officer on duty did not leave his place at the entrance to the small building when he spoke to me. "Where did you come from at this time of night?"

"From just over there," I answered.

"And where, exactly, is 'over there'?"

"From over by the moat."

"What moat?"

"There's a river called Yamaya, it runs by Matsuchiyama."

"What's your name?"

"Tadasu Oe," I answered, to which the policemen responded by flipping open a notepad. I quickly explained the spelling of my name.

He glared at me throughout my explanation as if to say "shut up," and when he was finished noting my name he quickly unbuttoned my jacket and started turning it over in his hands.

"There's nothing here," he grunted, looking in the collar.

"What are you looking for?" I asked, leaning to show him the collar of my vest as well.

"What's your address?"

"Otan, 1-6 Azabu."

"What do you do for work?"

"Nothing in particular."

"Unemployed then. How old are you?"

"Year of the Rabbit in Yin."

"I said, how old are you?"

"Year of the Rabbit, 1879," I said with the intention of remaining silent, but I quickly worried over his reaction and, recanting, stated: "58."

"Still young aren't you?"

"Ahaha."

"And what did you say your name was?"

"I believe I just told you. Tadasu Oe."

"You have a family?"

"Three of us," I answered. It was a lie, I had no family, but in my experience people trusted you more if you said you had one. I'd adopted a custom of answering the question with "three."

"You say 'three,' so you have a wife and who else?"

He asked, interpreting my answer in the nicest way he could have.

"Wife and Ma."

"How old's your wife?"

The question gave me pause for a moment, but I quickly remembered a woman I'd once had a relationship with and answered, "31. Born in 1906, July 14th. Year of the horse."

Had he asked for her name I was ready to answer with the name of a character in the novel I was working on, but he said nothing. He patted down my overcoat and, finding a lump in the pocket asked, "What do you have in here?"

"A pipe and my glasses."

"Fine. What about down here?"

"Can of food."

"What about this? This a wallet? Why don't you pull it out and give me a look at it."

"There's money in there."

"How much?"

"Probably around 20 or 30 yen."

He took out the wallet but did not open it. He set it on the small table used to hold the phone and continued, "What's that package you've got there? Come on in and show me what's in it."

I untied the towel and he looked inside. There were no problems with the clump of bread or the old magazine, but the policeman altered his demeanor the moment he saw the long, seductive singlet sleeve.

He snorted. "What the hell is this? You're carrying some strange stuff, old man."

"Oh, that, ahahaha..." I laughed.

"What are ya carrying this for? It's awfully... *womanly*," he sneered, pinching the singlet with revulsion between his fingers and holding it up to the light. He snapped his eyes back on me, and snorted, "Where'd you get this?"

"At a secondhand shop."

"Why do you have it?"

"I bought it with the money from my wallet. Opened the wallet up and bought it."

"And where was this?"

"By the large gate in Yoshiwara."

"How much did you pay for it?"

"Three yen and seventy sen."

He threw the singlet on the table and glared at me in silence. It seemed as though he was deciding whether or not to throw me in the pen with the other criminals, and in the face of such consideration the courage necessary for my previous lighthearted jesting quickly abandoned me. I watched him in silence, just as he watched me. His eyes moved down to my wallet, which he flipped open and started perusing. Inside he discovered a long-forgotten temporary certificate for fire insurance, a certificate from city hall for the registration of my seal, which of course was accompanied by the seal itself. He went through the papers one by one, unfolding them, flattening out the creases and laying them neatly on top of one another, proceeding to inspect my seal by the light. He peered, brow furrowed, at the relief of my name carved into the end. One could not accuse him of a lack of professional rigor. I passed the time by standing in the doorway and gazing out into the street.

The road split diagonally in two directions just in front of the police box; one led off towards South Senju, the other towards Shirahige Bridge. Before it split the road stretched out from the backside of Asakusa Park and crossed the major traffic artery that lead to Kototoi Bridge. Even at night the area was usually filled with a fairly constant traffic flow, though perhaps due to the odd and unsettling look of my doorway questioning, no pedestrians opted to linger within earshot. There was a shirt shop across the street, and the woman running it, shopboy at her side, was starting over in my direction, disinterested, as she closed up the shop.

"Hey, that's enough, put all this stuff away

already."

"None of these things are really very important anyway," I whispered as I collected my wallet and carefully retied the handkerchief around my things. "Do you need anything else?"

"No."

"Have a nice night then," I said, pulling out a gold-tipped Westminster cigarette and bringing a match to the tip. At the very least, the policeman deserved a good sniff of the scent, so before I turned and strode toward Kototoi Bridge, I turned back and exhaled a heavy lungful of smoke into the police box.

In hindsight, I am struck by the revelation that, had my seal and its certification not been tucked into my wallet, he most certainly would have thrown me into the pen. Good lord, secondhand clothes are unsettling things. That worn-out scrap of cloth was a curse.

Chapter Two

I have outlined a new idea for a novel I intend to call *Disappearance*. If I were to actually write it—and do afford me this small indulgence—I have a fair amount of confidence that it would not be intolerably terrible.

The protagonist will be called Junbei Taneda. He is a little over 50 years old, and is employed as an English teacher at a private middle school. At the start of the story it has been three or four years since Junbei lost his wife and became a widower. Soon he meets Mitsuko, whom he will remarry.

Mitsuko was employed at a certain famous politician's estate, where she was the personal maid of the politician's wife. However, she was deceived by the owner of the estate and became pregnant. The politician asked a butler who saw to his affairs, a certain Endo, to attend to the matter. If Mitsuko complied with the estate owner's requests he promised to send her five yen every month, for the first 20 years of the child's life, to secure the child's wellbeing. In return Mitsuko was never to mention the child in connection to his name, and he was never to be declared the father or included in any official documentation. There was also talk, in the event that Mitsuko was to marry, of awarding the family an impressive dowry.

So Mitsuko left to stay with Endo, the butler, and gave birth to a baby boy. In the space of two months, through the mediation of Endo, she found herself married to Junbei, the middle school English teacher. At the time she was 19. Junbei was 30.

Since losing his first wife, Junbei had been living on a small salary and was unable to perceive hope around him. As middle age approached he became sluggish and exhausted, a shadow of a man, but after talking with his friend Endo, he was momentarily enticed and confused at the mention of Mitsuko's money. Soon they were married.

Because the child had been born so recently,

Mitsuko had yet to file the proper documentation. With consideration to their marriage, Endo arranged to have both Mitsuko and the child registered officially on Junbei's family records. If one were to look into their records, it would have appeared as though they had been in a common-law marriage, and only decided to register with the state due to the birth of their son.

Two years went by, and Mitsuko gave birth to a daughter. Soon after, they had another son.

Their oldest son, who was not Junbei's, soon reached the age where it was time for him to set out on his own, at which point a letter suddenly arrived from the politician. His monthly payments were to be cut off. It was not just that the agreed-upon timeframe had passed. In fact, the actual father had died of a terrible illness, and shortly after his wife followed him to the grave.

Their oldest daughter Hoko was raised much as second children often are—her allowance was raised ever higher by the year. Eventually Junbei was forced to take on two or three night jobs to cover their expenses.

The oldest son, while studying at a private college, became an athlete and soon went overseas. The oldest daughter Hoko, became active in theater circles and found herself a sort of star actress from nearly the moment she graduated from her girl's school.

Mitsuko, who'd had a charming, rounded face at the time of their marriage, grew heavier with time, and the lines on her face stretched into the crevices and wrinkles of an old woman. She became deeply invested in a school of Buddhism, the Nichirenshu, and eventually became a member of their managing body.

Junbei spent his time teaching, and finding moments between his lessons to run back and forth to theaters and athletic fields to wish his children well and participate in the formal greeting of their superiors. The house was always in such an uproar of activity that even the mice were afraid to poke their noses from their holes at night.

Junbei had, ever since his childhood, a low tolerance for socializing and noise, and with age that tolerance was tried by the incessant hustle and bustle in his own home. He discovered an unaffected scorn for all of Mitsuko's beloved things. He made a concerted effort to suffer his family, but his need for revenge found manifestation in the cold look he often gave his wife. There was no other way for a soft-spoken man like himself to behave.

Junbei quit his job in the spring of his 51st year. On the day of his retirement he did not go home. He disappeared and told no one where he was going.

One day, on the train, he randomly met a girl who had once worked at his home as a maid. Her name was Sumiko, and as it turned out she was employed at a cafe in Asakusa. Junbei went there a few times and got tipsy on beer.

After sometime had passed he received his retirement severance pay, which he quickly stashed in his pocket and made for Sumiko's apartment, told her of his situation, and spent the night...

*   *   *

I am not sure how to end the story.

His family will put out a missing persons report. A detective will track him down and force an explanation out of him. These pleasures, pursued late in life, are often likened to rain just before twilight. I could make his end as miserable as I saw fit.

I have thought of many ways for Junbei to fall, and of the emotions that would accompany that fall. But I am still undecided as to the course he should take. I've thought about how it would feel for him to be handcuffed and taken away by the detective. I've thought about how it would feel for him to be given back over to his wife, the embarrassment and shame of it. How would it feel to be put in that situation?

When I bought the tattered singlet in the back alley of Sanya, I was taken in by the police and had my background thoroughly investigated. That experience will prove incredibly instructive in my effort to describe the state of Junbei's mind.

When composing a novel I find the time when the characters make choices that will affect their lives and lead to the development of events to be the most interesting. Those moments of development and their descriptions are fascinating. Conversely, I have also fallen into the trap of placing to much weight and descriptions on the sets and the background when I should have been focusing on the characters and their personalities.

I developed Junbei's story from a desire to depict Tokyo, and how its old lovely streets lost their individuality and beauty in the post-earthquake reconstruction. To that end Junbei will, no doubt, hide out in Honjo or Fukakawa or on the outskirts of Asakusa, or even hidden in an alleyway further to the east in those lands that had been farms until but a few years before.

Up until this point I have, on my occasional walks, intended to give a flavor of the life around Suna, Kamedo, Komatsugawa, and Terajima, but when it comes time for me to put down my brush, I feel as though my descriptions lack some effect. At one point (near the turn of the century), I composed a novel about the brothels of Fukagawa Asaki, and when I showed it to a friend of mine his reaction was, "You cannot hope to capture the feeling of the Asaki brothel towns without putting in something about the torrential rains of August and September. You know the tower of the very building you speak of has blown down once or twice in those incredible storms." To precisely capture the background of the story, attention must be given to the seasons and the climate. The great Lafcadio Hearn did so elegantly in his *Chita* and *Youma*.

It was an evening in June. The season of heavy rains was not over yet, but the sky had been clear since morning. I finished my dinner while the shadows were still long across the street. Twilight showed no sign of descending. I put down my chopsticks and left the shop with plans to walk far out to Senju or Kameido or wherever my feet felt like taking me, and with that intention I caught a streetcar to Kaminarimon, which just so happened to arrive concurrently with a bus on its way Tamanoi, on the other side of the river.

We crossed Azuma Bridge and turned left on the wide street. We crossed Genmori Bridge and went straight on past Akiha Shrine, which brought us to a set of train tracks, where the car came to a stop at the gate. Taxis and cars lined up on either side of the tracks and waited for the train to slowly rumble by. There were few people out walking, but there were crowds of children from the poor houses, hordes of them, playing games in the streets. I got off the streetcar where the wide road running from Shirahige Bridge to Kameido reached a large intersection. There were open lots filled with ragged patches of grass. They sat among the low rows of houses that lined the streets. The streets went on and on and all looked so similar that you could never tell them apart. No matter where I went, the streets exuded a loneliness, a quiet sadness.

If Junbei ran from his family and hid out in one of the alleys of this town, he'd be near the Tamanoi grounds. That might make the story easier to end. I played with the idea as I went on about a block and turned into a narrow alleyway. Vehicles or people carrying boxes had a hard time passing each other, it was so narrow, and every few feet it turned and winded through the buildings. On either side there were relatively nice little gates before relatively nice little rented houses and, occasionally, in the long stretches, I could catch glimpses of men and women in suits on their way home from work. The dogs had license numbers printed on their collars, and seemed well kept and clean. A moment later I came out of the alley just to the side of the Tobu line Tamanoi Station parking lot.

On either side of the tracks stood large trees,

manicured lawns, and what I could only assume were summer homes. There had been no places like this on my way here from Azuma Bridge. None of them looked as though they had been attended to in a while, and the ivy creeping across them and over the bamboo groves pulled the scene down with an extraordinary weight. The hedges lining the ditches were filled with moonflower blossoms, which lent such an extraordinary air of refinement that I was stopped in my tracks to gaze at them.

I recalled suddenly that the area around the Shirahige Shrine had once been known as Terajima Village. I could suddenly picture one of those estates as belonging to Kikugoro, the great Kabuki actor. The sight of the gardens, left long unattended, brought the elegant pursuit of artistry of that age back to the fore of my mind.

The train tracks were lined on one side by an expanse of open plots, stuck here and there with signs indicating they were for sale. They extended out to the river embankment where they met with an old steel bridge.

It had been part of the Keisei Electric Railway until just last year. At the top of the crumbling stone steps sat the old Tamanoi train stop, now overgrown with weeds. When viewed from a distance it towered over the town like an ancient castle, lost to time.

I pushed aside the high grass and climbed up the hillside of the embankment. There were no objects to obstruct my view of the street I'd just come up. The rambling old towns, empty lots, and developing areas could all be seen. On the other side of the river, corrugated iron roofs spread out in all directions, broken here and there by the towering chimneys of the baths, all of it cast in the glow of the setting summer sun. At one end of the sky the colors of sunset grew weaker and colder as they drifted away. The moon shone bright, as if night had already come. Between the iron roofs, in the gaps that showed the streets, neon signs crackled to life, and the echoes of radios clicking on here and there rose up from the town.

I sat on a stone until darkness fell, but soon all the

lights came on in the windows under the embankment, lending me a clear view into the untidy workings of the second floor rooms. My footprints were still just visible between the grasses, and I followed them back down the embankment wall. The square surrounding Tamanoi, for at least a block, was filled with people bustling between the ever-expanding rows of shops. Glowing lanterns stood out over the streets and business. They were scrawled with messages of "Thru Street," "Safety First," "Keisei Bus Shortcut," "Girls Girls Girls," and "Nigiwaihon Street."

I took a stroll around to breathe in the surroundings before stopping at a little shop that stood behind a post box. I bought some tobacco, paid for it with a five-yen bill, and was waiting for change when it happened. A man in a white half-jacket ran barreling down the street and ducked into an oden shop, hollering "It's gonna pour!" as he pushed back the curtain. A second later the aproned women and people passing in the streets fell into an uproar rushing into shops and under cover. I had only a moment to wonder what the fuss was about before a sudden wind blew heavily down the street, carrying signs and fabrics with it. There was a sudden, great cacophony of things crashing to the ground. All the papers and garbage of the town were swept up in the sudden gust and rushed down the street like a monster. Shortly after came a sharp flash of lightning, a strobe in the distance, then the soft, rolling thunder came, and finally the heavy, large drops of rain. It had been so clear all day, only to change in an instant.

A habit has come to me over the years. I never leave the house without an umbrella. No matter how clear the sky may have looked when I stepped from my house, it was the rainy season and so, in keeping with my custom, I was carrying both an umbrella and a handkerchief that day. I was not surprised by the sudden downpour. I simply opened my umbrella and looked out at the sky and town from under its lip. I was making my way down the street, among the crashing globes of rain, when suddenly, from behind me, "Good sir! Won't you let me under there?" A woman, her neck powdered pure white, thrust her head under my umbrella. The scent of oil made clear that her high, Japanese-styled chignon had been freshly dressed. It was decorated with thin cords of silver. I recalled passing a hairdresser's shop, its glass doors had stood open.

The wind howled and brought sheets of rain down the street. There was something pitifully tragic about the thin silver cord coming loose from her neatly tied bun, so I held out my umbrella to her and said, "Go on—I'm in a suit so it doesn't matter if I get wet."

In truth, I was embarrassed to be seen sharing an umbrella with her there, in the light of the shops for all to see.

"Oh? Thank you! It's just over there," she said taking the handle of the umbrella. She rolled up the bottom of her robe and sleeves from the pooling puddles of rain.

Chapter Three

Lightning flashed in the sky, followed by the low rumble of thunder. In response the woman shouted an affected, "Oh, my!" and reached back to grab my hand (I'd made a point of walking a step or two behind her). "We need to hurry, dear," she said pulling at me, as if we'd known each other for years.

"It's fine, you walk ahead—I'm right behind you."

We turned down a winding alleyway, and with every turn she looked back to make sure I was still behind her. Eventually we crossed a little bridge and found ourselves before a strip of low buildings with signs and awnings. We splashed to a stop before one of the little houses.

"Oh, dear—look at you!" she shouted. "You're soaked through!" She quickly folded the umbrella away and saw to wiping the beaded water off of my shoulders before attending to herself.

"This your house?"

"I'll get you dry, come on inside."

"It's a suit, like I said; I'll be fine."

"Even though I'm offering to help? How am I supposed to show my gratitude?"

"Show your gratitude? What exactly did you have in mind?"

"Well... you'll see. Anyway, come on inside."

The lightning had moved off, but the rain was pouring harder than it had before. It pounded the street and raised a hissing mist over the roofs and signs. I hurried inside without further protest.

There was a partition in the middle of the room, covered with rough Osaka latticework and a rolling blind of ribbon. A little bell hung affixed to its strings. I took a seat on a bench that sat below the partition and, as I saw to remove my shoes, the woman finished wiping her feet with a spare cloth, unrolled her sleeves, and twisted the knob on a nearby electric lamp.

"There's no one here," she said. "Come on up."

"You alone here?"

"Yes. There was another person here until last night. They moved out."

"Your husband, I presume?"

"No. My *master* lives somewhere else. By chance do you know the theater in Tamanoi? He has a house just behind it. He usually stops by around midnight to check the books."

"Guess you can do whatever you want then," I said, taking the seat she offered me by the stove heater. She knelt at the table and began to prepare tea. I watched her.

I supposed she was around twenty-five. Her face was a pretty little thing. The skin on her straight nose and rounded face was slightly rough from the application of cosmetics, but her neatly dressed hair had the shine of youth. Her large black eyes were clear, and her lips and gums were pink with blood, young and healthy.

"Is it well or city water around here?" I asked absentmindedly before I drank my tea. Had she answered well water I would to pretend to take a sip and leave the cup undrunk. I was far more scared of a typhus infection then any sort of venereal disease. Old men such as myself, ruined spiritually far before we could lose out to our bodies, had little to fear from slow, chronic diseases

"Did you want to wash up? We have city water right over there," she said motioning off with postured amiability.

"Thanks, I might use it later."

"At least take off that jacket. It's soaked through."

"Sure is pouring out there."

"I'm more bothered by the flashing than by the thunder. At this rate I can't get near the baths. Dear, you're alright for a little while? I'd like to wash up and redo my makeup."

She twisted her lips up and patted at her hairline with strips of paper she pulled from a pocket and went to stand before the sink, which protruded from the wall on the other side of the partition. Between the slats in the partition I could see her pull off the top of her robe and wash her face. Her shoulders were much whiter than her face, and from the look of her breasts she had clearly never had a child.

"Aren't we casual? You'd think we were husband and wife here. And what a little home you've set up. You've got a bureau, tea shelves..."

She motioned with a languid finger. "You can open that if you'd like. There should be some potatoes or something in there."

"You keep it clean—I'm impressed. What's in the heater?"

"I clean every morning. It may be bit of a dump, but I like to think I keep it nice."

"Have you been here a long time?"

"About a year, maybe a little longer?"

"But you're not new to the area, are you? Were you

a geisha or something?"

I wasn't sure if she couldn't hear me over the sound of the bubbling water or if she had simply feigned a sudden auditory impairment, but she said nothing, just sat down in front of the mirror, still undressed. She pulled her hair up and began powdering her shoulders.

"Where'd you come from? You can't just keep that secret."

"I know... but it wasn't Tokyo."

"The suburbs?"

"No, much further..."

"China?"

"I was in Utsunomiya. All my kimonos are from thereabouts too. I'd rather not talk about it." She stood up and pulled on a robe that had been hanging on a hook. The under-sash was lined with thin red stripes and finished with a large knot in the front, which was just large enough to give balance to her nearly oversized chignon with its silver threads. She appeared to me just as a courtesan from a previous age. She sat down beside me and fiddled with her robe until it was just right before opening a package of cigarettes.

"We're already here, so the amount doesn't matter. But do see to it that you show your appreciation, just to keep up appearances." She passed me a lit cigarette.

I couldn't claim total ignorance of the area's reputation. "50 sen for the tea, isn't it?"

"Naturally. I'd say that's about standard," she said with a smile. She moved her hand closer to mine.

"Well, let's decide on a time. About an hour?"

"It just doesn't seem right. I'm terribly sorry about all this—really I am."

"Well, in exchange..." I said and took her hand. I pulled her close to me and whispered in her ear.

"I don't know about that!" she glared at me, eyes blazing, and slapped my shoulder. "Dummy."

Readers of Tamenaga Shunsui will be familiar with the author's tendency to break from his narrative to apologize on behalf of himself or his characters. So when a young girl, hopelessly in love for the first time, forgets her shame and throws herself at the man she loves, the author interjects on her behalf and warns the reader not to think her a harlot or flippant. Indeed, he says, the simple girl, when deeply in love, can move with the allure and seduction of a geisha. Furthermore, the world-weary professional woman, well known in the ways of love, can, upon an encounter with a childhood friend, squirm and blush like a fresh faced virgin.

Anyone with sufficient experience in such matters can attest to the truth of his statements, and I would not be one to declare his observations deficient.

Taking a cue from Shunsui, I will elaborate further here, perhaps more than necessary. The reader may note my description of this woman, and the overly familiar way she behaved upon meeting me in the street. The reader might find this odd, even suspicious. But I would beg the reader keep in mind one thing: I have simply stated exactly what happened when we met, with absolutely no elaboration on my behalf. I have no unscrupulous intentions. There may even be a reader or two who smirks to themselves upon reading my account of what occurred just after the sudden downpour on that day. However, due to my desire to give proper and true consideration to the preceding events, I would not wish to build castles in the air for my enjoyment. But what happened that night, just as the sun went down, was so traditional, so conventional, that truthfully I can find nothing of interest to say about it.

In truth, the reason I began to write this very text you hold in your hands was to see if I could find the interest in the action.

The brothel women in that town must have numbered near eight hundred, but probably only one in ten had their hair tied up in elaborate chignons. Most of them dress up in an imitation of traditional Japanese style, some of them affect the air of a western dancer. This woman, the one who ran to get out of the rain, belonged to the small group of them who carried on the old ways, but even my attempts to describe her seem trite, hackneyed, and affected. I cannot avoid doing the description harm.

The rain didn't stop.

When she first let me into the house it was raining so hard that I'd had to raise my voice to be heard over the din, but the wind howling at the door and the booming thunder had died off, leaving only the sound of the raindrops battering the roof and the heavy drops pooling and dripping to the ground. For the first time in a while the street was cleared of people's chattering and the sounds of their feet on the pavement, and then, suddenly:

"Oh, dear!" came the shriek of a passing woman. "There are guppies swimming around out here!"

The woman stood up and peeked out between the ribbons. "The house is fine. If the embankment overflows the water will come up to here."

"Sounds like it's letting up a bit."

"If it pours in the evening like this then it doesn't matter if it clears up. Please just make yourself at home. I'm going to go ahead and eat."

She opened the tea shelves and pulled out some pickled radishes, which she piled on a plate before reaching in again and taking out some bowls and a little aluminum pot. She removed the lid and tentatively sniffed the interior of the pot before setting it, satisfied, on the brazier. A sideways glance showed the pot was filled with sweet potatoes.

"Hey now—I'd forgotten. I've got something good here," I said rummaging through my things. When I had changed trains at Kyobashi, I'd bought a package of dried Asakusa seaweed. I pulled it out and passed it to her.

"You must have bought it for your wife," she said.

"I'm not married. I need to do my own shopping."

"Then you must live in an apartment with your girlfriend," she giggled.

"If that was true I wouldn't be hanging around

here. I'd have gone home a while ago, to hell with the rain and thunder."

"I suppose so." She smiled contentedly to herself, as if she approved of my response. The pot was warming up, so she pulled off the lid and peeked inside. "Care to have some with me?"

"I already ate."

"Then turn and look over that way."

"You cook your own rice?"

"They bring it from the main house at lunch time and at midnight."

"What do you say we make some new tea? It's gone cold."

"Oh, dear, that wasn't very hospitable of me was it? Tell me something," she said. "You like to have conversations over dinner?"

"It's preferable to eating alone."

"Oh, come now. You mean you really are all alone? You poor thing!"

"Spare me your sympathy."

"It's fine, I'll find you some."

She made two bowls of tea rice. She seemed excited, giddy, as she carefully placed the chopsticks over the bowls before hurrying to put the small plates and pots back in the tea cabinet. She rolled her chin back and forth as if trying to keep down a radish-smelling burp.

Outside the door came the sound of feet on pavement and the raucous laughter of a man.

"Looks like the rain has stopped. I'd like to come by again someday soon."

"Please do. I'm here in the afternoon too."

She saw me pull on my coat and soon she had rushed behind me and straightened my collar. She set her cheek on my shoulder. "See you soon then."

"What's the address?"

"I've got a card. Hold on a minute."

When I was pulling on my shoes she rushed to the small window, where there was a box sitting. From the box she produced a small card, in the shape of a shamisen pick. The address said Terajima, 7-chome, No. 61, and her name was Yukiko Ando.

"Goodbye."

"Head straight home."

Chapter Four

An excerpt from *Disappearance*:

Near the center of Azuma Bridge, Junbei Taneda pressed himself against the railing and gazed at the Matsuya clock. His mind was on the people passing him. He was waiting for Sumiko, who would come to meet him after she closed up her shop. He made sure to take the long way around to meet her.

The bridge was free of taxis, trains, and buses, but there were some people walking by (in short, thin shirts to fight off the warming days), and the girls had bundles tucked under their arms, probably on their way home. Junbei planned to spend the night at Sumiko's apartment and use the time to consider where he would go next. He had not thought of what the woman would do after he left, and he didn't have the time or composure to think of it now. All he could think of was the 20 years of his life, up until that point, that he had wasted on his family. A boiling discontent stirred within him.

"Sorry to keep you waiting!" Sumiko trotted over much earlier than expected. "I normally come by Komagata Bridge, but I was with Kaneko today. She can be so annoying."

"I think the trains have stopped."

"It's only three stops or so. But we can catch a taxi over there."

"I hope they have a room."

"If not, why don't you just stay at my place tonight?"

"You sure that's okay?"

"Don't think anything of it."

"But don't you see those articles in the paper? So-and-so caught in an apartment..."

"That depends where you are. I'm sure of it. I have a lot of freedom at my place. The girls beside and across from me both work the brothels. I see people coming and going from the girl next door's place all the time."

Before they finished crossing the bridge they picked up a taxi for Akiha Shrine. They agreed to 30 sen.

"This area sure has changed. How far does the train go now?"

"Mukojima. Right in front of Akiha. The buses go all the way out to Tamanoi though."

"Tamanoi…That was just down that way, right?"

"Exactly."

"I went there once. Just for some sightseeing. Must have been five or six years ago."

"It's a great place. Bustling. They set up shops every night and even put on shows in the fields."

"You don't say."

Junbei watched the towns slide by the car window, and soon the vehicle came to a stop in front of the Akiha Shrine. Sumiko pulled at the door handle.

"This is just fine. Right," she said, passing a pinch of change to the driver. "Let's turn in down there. Better to stay away from that police box."

They followed the stone wall of the shrine around a corner and Junbei found himself in a small alleyway, lined on both sides with lanterns covered in the names of various brothels. At the darkened corner of a large, empty lot stood a square cement building. A lantern lit the front. *Azuma* Apartments was scrawled over the paper. Sumiko slid the door open, stepped inside, brushed off her shoes, and slid them into a box with a number that matched that of her apartment. Junbei made to do the same when she stopped him.

"Let's bring them upstairs. Someone will notice them here."

She passed him her own slippers and, slipping her fingers between the thongs of his wooden shoes, hurried up the stairwell.

The walls and windows looked western-styled, but the interior pillars were thin and rounded in the Japanese style. The softly creaking stairs led to a hallway, at the corner of which was a small kitchen. A woman in a slip was drying her hair and filling a kettle on the stove with water.

Sumiko gave her a polite, "Evening," and turned a key to open the second-to-last door on the right.

It was a small room with dirtied tatami mats. One wall was dedicated to the closet, while at another stood a wardrobe. The remaining wall was covered with hanging bathrobes and nightgowns. Sumiko slid a window open. "It's cool here." She set out cushions. Socks and belts hung from the window.

"It must be nice to live this way. It must be free. Makes marriage look ridiculous by comparison."

"They keep asking me to come back home. But I can't do that anymore."

"If only I'd come to my senses earlier. It's too late now," said Junbei as he set his weight against the windowsill and gazed out at the sky. And then, as if he suddenly remembered it, he asked "Can you ask if they have any open rooms?"

Sumiko appeared as though she was waiting to prepare the tea. She stepped out into the hallway to get the hot water and paused. She spoke to another woman and hurried back into the room.

"Sounds like the room across the hall is open. But the landlord isn't here tonight."

"So I suppose they won't rent it out to me? Tonight I mean."

"Why not stay here for a night or two? As long as you're not bothered by it."

Junbei was taken aback. "I'm fine, but what will you do?"

"I'll sleep here. Or I can go next door for the night. As long as her boyfriend isn't staying over."

"No one comes here looking for you?"

"Nope, at least not yet. So I don't mind you staying. Of course, I wouldn't want to expose you to any unwanted… temptation."

Junbei's face quickly went through a series of

contortions, as if he wanted to laugh, then as if he was very sad and shamed. He said nothing.

"You say you have a wife and daughter after all..."

"I'm not worried about that kind of thing. I'm starting over now. A new life."

"You'll live separately?"

"Yes, or just separate completely."

"You know that doesn't go over very well most of the time."

"That's why I'm thinking it over. I don't care if it involves a little violence, I just need to disappear for a little while. If I can do that I'm sure I'll find a way out of all this. Listen, Sumiko—if there aren't any open rooms then I don't want to put you out. I'll go find another place to stay tonight. Why don't we go look around the town?"

She paused. "I have something I'd like to discuss too. I'm worried about something, and I don't know what to do. Can't you just stay up talking with me tonight?"

"Dawn is coming earlier and earlier this time of

year."

"I went for a drive out to Yokohama recently. The sun was already coming up by the time we made it home."

"If we talk about all that, from the beginning, it must have been tough for you to work as a maid at my house. Not to mention all that you must have been through since you started your new... profession."

"That's true. We might not get through all of it in one night," she laughed.

The second floor had been nearly silent the whole time, but suddenly the voices of a man and woman came floating down the hall, along with the sloshing of water down by the kitchen. Sumiko appeared set on talking the whole night through. She unwrapped her belt and neatly folded it before removing her socks and filing them away in the closet. She wiped the table down with a cloth until it was spotless and began to brew tea before speaking. "And why do you think it is that I've chosen this life?"

"I don't know. I suppose you had always harbored

an interest in the work?"

"Well, I suppose there was a little bit of that. But there were other motivators. I *despise* my father's business."

"Which was?"

"He likes to say he takes care of people, he thinks himself valorous," she said, lowering her voice to a whisper. "Anyway, he runs some sort of gang..."

Chapter Five

The rainy season came to an end with an oppressive wave of heat, and perhaps it was because every single door of every single house stood open to try and fight it that normally unnoticed sounds seemed to fill the hot air. Among these sounds, none gave me more trouble that the persistent sound of the radio, which emanated from my neighbor's house. We were separated only by a thin, wooden fence.

Waiting for the evening air to cool, I made to sit at my desk under the light when I was startled by the sudden, shrill sound of cracking and splitting from the speaker. It did not cease until past nine o clock. Among the noise came the blaring, obnoxious sound of political debate in the Kyushu accent, followed quickly by some type of drama read in the affected tone of a school play. The producers had mixed in western orchestration to 'enrich' the drama.

As if the sound of the radio was not enough to satisfy them, plenty of other houses blared popular songs from their gramophones. Whenever summer comes and the doors slide open, to spare myself the annoyance of their cacophony, I have made a point of eating my dinners early, or skipping them all together, and leaving my house when six o' clock draws near. This is not to imply that just leaving the house will get me far enough away from the radios to spare my ears their wretched influence. Putting some distance between them and myself may spare me the intensity of people's radios and the bustling of shops, but it is replaced by the chugging of trains and the whirring of cars to the extent that the whole town seems to be buzzing and clicking with noise. Yes, the noise is there, but compared to sitting alone in my study, I find that it doesn't bother me so much when I am walking. It's actually quite nice.

My work on the *Disappearance* manuscript ceased with the end of the rains and the emergence of the radios.

It had been ten days since I gave it up. I could feel my interest evaporating.

This year, just as last year and the year before that, I left my house while the sun still hung on the horizon, but my walks were directionless. When Kojiro was alive I would have gone to Ginza, so cool at night, and I could have spend the whole night there without running out of things to see. But he has already passed on, and the lights of Ginza no longer hold my interest. Furthermore, there was an event that led me to avoid Ginza on my aimless wanderings. Before the earthquake there was a rickshaw driver who showed his face in all the geisha houses, and it was a face like a murderer—disheveled and snarling. He got along with no one, and bullied others. He wandered the streets of Owari and when he saw a face he remembered from somewhere he chased them down and pestered them relentlessly for money.

Once, when this business had just started, I ran into him in front of Kurosawa's and I gave him 50 yen. The

kindness proved to be a mistake, after which he was sure
to cause a scene the next time we met if I refused him
another 50. I gave it to him once more. Moreover, it seemed
I wasn't the only one buying him drinks. Thinking it over,
I once tricked him into accompanying me not to a bar, but
to a police box down the street. The officers on duty were
apparently old friends of his though, and they made no
effort to assist me. Another time I saw him laughing with
the officers at the police box in Izumo... but no, they've
gone and renamed that area now. I believe it's called the
7th district now. Regardless, the police seemed to prefer
his company to mine.

I altered my path and made for the east side of the
Sumida River, thinking I would pay another visit to Yukiko
Ando, whom I had taken to calling Oyuki, at her house by
the embankment and relax there for a spell.

After walking the path back and forth for five days
or so, it was an easy walk—easier than my first long walk
from Azabu. I changed trains at Kyobashi and

Kaminarimon, and it became a habit, the sort that your body moves on its own before your conscious mind has time to step in and regulate. The automation made the distance less bothersome. The trains fill up with people at different times each day, but once you've got it figured out you can avoid the rush, and even long distances become opportunities, not only for transport, but for quiet reflection over a book.

Sometime around 1920, I began to need glasses for my reading, at which point I completely gave up on reading on the trains. But now, with the long round trip from Kaminarimon, I decided to take up my old habit again. However, it has never been a custom of mine to reach for newspapers, magazines, or recently published books, and in keeping with my private custom the first book I brought with me was Gakukai Yoda's *Twenty-four scenes of the Sumida.*

Rolling, squirming riverbank.

A bow, strung with three shrines.

Ending at Chomei (long life) Temple.

Blanketed with cherry blossoms.

The Tokugawas once loosed falcons here.

A sip of its waters

Can sure the stomach's ills.

The water of long life,

hence the temple's appellation.

Basho wrote of its snows,

So loved by the people.

A hero for the ages,

his name shook the earth's foundations.

The robe of a monk is no more than a strip of cloth,

but they say that if you stood before this tree,

you could hear him.

I hoped the old text would deepen my appreciation
for the scenes before me.

On my third trip I had to stop to buy some food on

the way. Considering I was already involved in a transaction, I decided to add something to the bill for the woman as well. I only made the trip four or five times, but the journey produced two tangible effects.

It was not just my diet of tin-canned foods, but also my occasionally shoddy appearance, say, a missing button on a jacket, that eventually convinced the woman that I really did live alone in an apartment. It follows then, that there is nothing particularly odd about a man going out on the town every night, so long as he is single. Surely no one would guess that I needed to vacate my apartment to escape the radios, and furthermore, if I did not go to see plays or motion pictures, then how else was I to spend my time? I was certain she did not think I came because I had nowhere else to go. Eventually I came to worry whether or not there were concerns about where my money came from, considering the area's reputation. I eventually asked her what she thought of it. She replied that as long as I paid her what was owed each night, that she was not concerned with anything else.

She explained further. "All sorts of people hang around here. We once had a customer who stayed an entire month."

"You don't say," I said, surprised. "Don't they need to inform the police? In Yoshiwara I heard that they have to tell the police all the time."

"Around here I'd say it depends on the apartment block."

"Who was it that stayed for a month? Some kind of thief?"

"He was from a kimono shop. Eventually the owner of the shop came in and dragged him off."

"Guess he ran off with the shop's money?"

"Probably."

"Well, you don't need to worry about me," I said to comfort her, but she appeared unconcerned to the point of apathy. She let the topic fade off.

With time, however, I came to realize that she had

come up with her own theories as to the source of my funds.

On the wall of the second floor alcove, there stands a very large frame filled with various ukiyo-e prints of beautiful women, all quarter-size reproductions. I had seen a few of them before as illustrations in magazines. Utamaro's *Abalone Divers*, Toyokuni's *Women of the Baths*, and so forth. There was also an altered print from Hokusai's three-volume erotic works, of which the man had been cut from the print, leaving only the woman. I explained the alteration in detail.

The explanation, along with the fact that I often wrote in my notebook while Oyuki was upstairs with clients (a practice that led to her often catching me unawares in the middle of my scribbles), combined in her mind and distilled into a theory in which I was involved in the publishing of "secret" books and materials. She asked me to bring one such book the next time I came.

I'd kept some old copies of collections from the past few decades, so I brought three or four of them along with me the next time, as requested. And so it came to be that, without ever speaking of my occupation, Oyuki not only decided that I was a publisher of such materials, but set her mind at ease about the supposed source of my income, and in doing so quickly changed her attitude towards me. As if letting down her hair, or rubbing the tension from her shoulders, she no longer treated me like a simple customer.

When the women who live in the shadows face the men who creep about in the darkness, there is no fear or malice in them, only kindness and love. There is no need for explanation; the innumerable acts speak for themselves, and nothing I put to paper can elaborate on them. There was the geisha from Kyoto who helped the man sought by the shoganate, the girl at the frigid train stop who emptied her pockets to help a gambler. Tosca fed the fugitive, Michitose gave all her love to the desperate man.

My greatest anxiety was the possibility of running into other writers or reporters around town, or possibly on the train. It does not matter in the least where I meet other

people. I had long since been cast off by the upstanding
aristocracy of the world. The children of my relatives no
longer came to see me. My only fear was of those other
scribes of the city. Once, some ten years prior, when cafes
were sprouting up all about Ginza, I'd had too much to
drink and drawn the attention of all the newspapers in
town. In April of 1929 the *Bungei Shunju* paper attacked
me as an "existence that needn't be tolerated." They
proceeded to depict my character as a "seducer of maidens,"
in an attempt, I can only imagine, to make me out as some
sort of criminal. To think of the articles they would pen
upon the discovery of my jaunts east of the river.

    I rode the train out there each night, and stole into
town. The main street was bustling at night with people
and the lit, buzzing signs of the shops. When the lanes and
alleyways are filled with people I need to keep a constant
watch over who is walking around me—both front, back,
left, and right. I believe the experience is essential, for if I
am to give an authentic description of hiding from the

world, I must deepen my understanding of Junbei Taneda, the protagonist of *Disappearance*.

Chapter Six

I have already indicated the whereabouts of the
house I sneak off to by the embankment: Terajima,
7-chome, No. 60-something. The block stands just up in the
northwest corner of the square, by which it follows that it
is not the best place to avoid prying eyes. If one were to
find a similar area in Yoshiwara, it would perhaps be in
Kyomachi, just to the side of the moat.

Allow me a slight digression regarding the evolving
nature of this area. In 1918, the area behind the Asakusa
Kannon Temple was made narrower by the construction of
a wide main road, but for many many years the area had
been filled with bars and various forms of entertainment,
and the businesses were forced out by the expanding road.
The businesses moved and now line both sides of Taisho
Street, which is plied by the Keisei buses daily. Those
businesses, along with ones relegated to behind Denbo-in

temple and Edo river Tama, now fill in nearly every available spot on Taisho Street. The hustle brought out the crooks, who grew so emboldened as to snatch the hats from people's heads in broad daylight, in response to which the police placed an ever more stringent watch on the area until the disreputable places were forced into alleyways where they could not be seen by passing cars. Back in the Asakusa area the shops behind Ryounkaku Tower in Senzoku did their damnedest just to stay afloat—an effort to which the earthquake and fires of 1923 laid waste, their inhabitants shuffled to this very same district for a time. Many of them quickly altered their lifestyles to approximate their new surroundings, and by the time the city was rebuilt they had formed unions and made geisha houses. Their newfound business interests brought prosperity to the town, along with which came the quasi-permanent status of the town. The only road from Tokyo into the town came across the Shirahige Bridge, which was crossed by the Keisei Electric Railway. Prior to the discontinuation of the line the most prosperous area was the streets surrounding the station.

Furthermore, in the spring of 1930, the city executed their plans to build a road connecting Azuma Bridge with Terajima. The city trains ran to Akiha Shrine, and the city bus routes were extended out to Terajima, 7-chome. At nearly the same time, the Tobu Railway Company constructed the Tamanoi Station just to the southwest of the main square so that people could come from Kaminarimon for just six sen. The sudden influx of people changed the face and backside of the town dramatically. What had previously been obtuse and nonnavigable alleyways became bright, welcoming thoroughfares, and what had previously been overlooked, though now on the outskirts of town, was crowded with banks, post offices, baths, theaters, cinemas, and the Tamanoi Inari Shrine still lined the main thoroughfare just as they always had. The new street, referred to as the "big little street" or the "redone street" was congested with taxis and night stalls. It was perhaps the busiest section of town, though despite its reputation it had yet to lay claim to a police box, or even a public toilet.

Even this backwater town, suddenly enlivened, was not able to escape the undulating and manic altercations of the times. And neither can any of us.

That house by the embankment, the one that set my mind at ease... The house where Oyuki lived stood at the corner of the district that exploded in popularity with the Taisho-era improvements. It felt, to someone like me, left behind by the times, as if we were connected by a deep, mysterious fate. To get there I would turn off of Taisho Street into an alleyway, walk past the Inari Shrine and its dirtied flags, find the embankment and walk alongside it further and further back until the sound of the radios and record players and footsteps disappeared and everything was silence again. In the summer, there was no place more suitable for escape from the radios. It was a place of rest.

The neighborhood had, as a rule by the local association, prohibited the playing of radios and gramophones from four o'clock in the afternoon, when the women would sit in the windows. They had banned the playing of the shamisen. With the rain and the deepening of night the calls of women for men grew less frequent, along with which the growing silence was filled with the drone from clouds of mosquitos filling the rooms. The sounds gave voice to the loneliness of these back alleys in a forgotten district. But it was not a twentieth-century sadness. It was the sadness one might find in the kabuki of Tsuruya Nanboku.

Oyuki, her hair in a looping chignon, framed with a view of the dirty embankment and surrounded by the murmur of mosquitos, always excited my senses. She brought the fading, phantom-like image of a world 30 years past back to vivid life. I wished I could find the words to express my gratitude to the one who brought that suspicious specter of the past back to me. Oyuki, far more

than the actresses, far more than the poets and their words
of butterflies, was an artist of exquisite refinement. She
could reach into the yawning gaps of time and bring the
past back to life.

As Oyuki slowly scoops rice from its basket to our
bowls, and then with the dribbling of tea over rice, along
with the dim electric light and the hum of the mosquitos—
when it all comes at once I can see those girls that I had
loved in my youth appear before my eyes, as if they were
there in the flesh. Back then we were not concerned with
fashionable words like "boyfriend" and "girlfriend," and
the preposterous title of "love nest" was never conferred
upon a place of common use. Husbands and wives referred
to one another with far less formality back then.

The mosquitos still drone over the embankment,
but if you cross the Sumida River and head to the east, it's
as though nothing has changed in 30 years. Their song is
of the melancholy reaches of the town. How great, even
these ten years, the change has been in the dialect of the

city!

The mosquito net, all folded up

The heat of the summer

The western, autumn sun, the embankments,

The pattering fans snap in half

in the autumn heat.

Tie off the holes in the mosquito nets.

It's the end of September.

The mosquitos come buzzing from the trash cans

You can seem them against the walls,

among the water splotches from the rains.

It's the start of autumn,

The mosquito nets and a bottle.

The above is an old song that came back to me one
day, while I was sitting in the tea room of Oyuki's

apartment and I noticed the hanging mosquito net by the window. Back then my friend Aa, long since passed, was living with a girl in secret, out behind the Fukagawa Chorei Temple. His parents didn't approve. I used to go out there to see him, so it must have been around 1910.

Oyuki poked her head out from the mosquito net and explained that she'd developed a sudden toothache that had kept her in bed all day. She had just been lying down. There was no place for her to sit so we lined up and sat on the step by the door.

"You're late. Oh, why do you have to keep me waiting?"

The woman's language and attitude had, with her presumed knowledge of my occupation, crossed the line from affectionate to nearly vulgar.

"I'm sorry. Is it a cavity?"

"It just started hurting. It hurts so badly I feel like the room is spinning. Is it swollen?" she asked, turning to show her profile. "Do me a favor, will you watch the room for me? I'd like to run to the dentist."

"Is it nearby?"

"Just over by the police."

"Then it must be near the public market."

"Well, well—you've walked all over this place so you certainly know it well. You cheater."

"Ouch. Don't be that way. I just do what I can to keep my head above water."

"Fine, then, I'm heading out. If it looks as though it will take too long I'll come straight back."

"Wait, wait, wait for me—but don't go under the mosquito net—is that how it is? Oh well, no matter."

I have made a point of matching my own demeanor to that of hers, so when she speaks roughly, I follow suit. This is not done in an effort to hide my true self, it is simply the way I choose to interact with modern people, no matter where they are from or who they are. Much like going overseas and taking the steps to speak the language of the land you are in, I try to match my diction to that of my conversation partner. In doing so I match my speech to that of the natives of foreign countries when I am there. When the partner becomes over-familiar, even rude, I find that I become the same. This digression grows long, but I might continue to say that when speaking with people in the modern dialect it is no problem for me to take on their tones, yet when it comes to writing letters I am overcome with difficulty in the endeavor. This is especially so with letters to women. Just how coy is one to behave on the page? This is to say little of the modern practice of attaching a "-ness" to words to increase their stature. "Inevitableness" and "importantness" and such rubbish. I often continue talking in said manner as a joke, but when it comes to lifting a brush and putting such words to paper I am overcome, time and again, with a fresh wave of revulsion.

The good things are those that will not return to us. Just the other day, when airing out my books, I'd come across an old letter from a geisha trained at Yanagibashi. She was in Koume then. Those were times when a certain degree of formality was expected in a letter, and despite perhaps not always knowing proper spellings, when she took up brush and ink she saw to it that her letter was true to form. At the risk of inviting ridicule, I should like to record her letter here.

"Please do understand that I wished to write you a letter. The duration of my silence has been far too long. I know it to be so and I am sorry. I also wish to inform you that I have moved to new quarters, as the state of my former rooms was in disarray. There is a matter that is difficult for me to give expression to in writing, but I simply must discuss it with you. At a time of your own convenience, do pay me a visit. I shall be waiting. Pardon the brevity of this letter, I am in an terrible hurry. I will tell you all of it when I see you. Please do hurry."

"Down by the ferry you will discover a boathouse. Ask the boy working there. The weather has been so nice lately, you might invite Aa to accompany you as well. It would be wonderful if the three of us could go to Horikiri.

Would it be easiest to make the trip in the morning? Pardon all these questions. Respond only if you feel inclined."

Many sentences carry distinct traces of a downtown woman's speech pattern. The Takeya Ferry is gone now. So is the Makurabashi Ferry. Where, then, am I to search out these sentimental relics of my youth?

Chapter Seven

After Oyuki left I spent the majority of my time sitting in the mosquito net, swatting at the mosquitos, occasionally adding charcoal to the brazier, occasionally boiling a pot of water. The heat of the evening was irrelevant; in this town it was customary to brew tea the moment a guest arrived. The houses were filled with flames and the bubbling of boiling water pots.

"Hey, psst!" someone whispered frantically and rapped on the window. Assuming it was one of Oyuki's customers, no doubt a hulking man, I quickly considered leaving, then hesitated, considered remaining, and was lost in the back and forth of my indecision when the man thrust the window open, flipped the latch with his thumb, and pressed his way into the room. He wore a white robe tied with a stiff belt and his coarse, unrefined, round face was covered by the creeping growth of a scraggly beard. He looked around 50. He held something bundled in a handkerchief. From the look of his stance and his face I quickly assumed he was Oyuki's boss. I didn't wait for him to speak. "Miss Oyuki had some kind of problem, she said she was going to the doctor. I just met her out front."

The boss-looking man acted as though he already knew. "She'll be back soon, I'm sure. Just wait for her." He did not appear to be concerned by my presence, and simply went about unwrapping his towel. Inside was a small aluminum pot, which he proceeded to place in the tea cabinet. It seemed he had brought her meal, which fixed it: he must have been her boss.

I wasn't sure what to say, so I opted for a roundabout compliment over a simple greeting. "Miss Oyuki sure is busy. She must be very popular."

"You think? Thanks," he gave a meaningless response as if he, too, was not sure how best to respond. He busied himself with attending to the coals and boiling water. He never faced me, or looked me in the eye. He seemed rather intent on avoiding conversation as much as possible. He turned away from me, and so, taking the cue, I remained silent.

The management of certain 'disreputable' businesses seems to have a very awkward time meeting the customers. Naturally it is awkward for the customer as well. Such meetings were likely nearly always unpleasant, and nearly always identical; they revolved around horrible disagreements over women.

Oyuki typically burned a mosquito coil by the door, but that day it appeared as though the coil had never been lit, as the room was filled with a thick cloud of mosquitos that were no longer satisfied with simply biting at my face, no—they took to batting at my mouth as well. The boss, whom I would have expected to be used to the area, sat still and tried to bear it for a moment or two before his patience wore thin and he dashed for the fan sitting in the corner of the room and twisted the knob. It must have been broken, because it did not move. He fished in a drawer for a moment, and when he triumphantly produced a large chip of mosquito coil from within we both let out contented sighs and finally he met my gaze. I took the opportunity to speak.

"The mosquitos are horrible this year—doesn't matter where you go. No doubt due to the heat. It's wretched."

He looked at me and drawled, "That so? Around here they don't build up the lots like they need to. Used to be a riverbank you know."

"But they sure built some nice roads. It certainly is more convenient than before."

"Sure, but 'cause of all that attention they are cracking down on the rules."

"Right, two or three years ago they'd snatch the hat off your head in broad daylight from what I hear."

"Bad times those were. Even if people had business out here they wouldn't come by. We warned the women, but of course we couldn't keep watch over them 24 hours a day. So we had to start fining them. So you run out in the street and try to lure in a man? Forty-two yen for that. We made a rule against using guys in the park too, lure in the customers, you know."

"There a fine for that too?"

He nodded.

"How much?"

I was planning on using these roundabout questions to learn a little more about the area when a man passed by the window and said, "Miss Ando," and dropped a scrap of paper into the room before continuing on his way. Oyuki came into the room at nearly the same time, picked up the paper, and set it on a board by the brazier. I stole a glance. It was a printed circular; the police were looking for a man on breaking and entering charges.

Oyuki did not even look at it. "Pops," she said, turning to the man. "They say I have to have it taken out tomorrow." She opened her mouth and showed the tooth to the man.

"Guess you didn't need dinner tonight then, huh?" He said as he stood. He then purposefully turned, just so that I could see him, before producing a quantity of money, handing it to Oyuki, and walking up the stairs to the second floor.

The second floor consisted of a very small room with a window and a tea table, one average bedroom, and one other very small nook. The house was so small, I assumed that it must have been larger in the past, but was split vertically down the center. The first floor was simply a tea room and a kitchen. There was no back door. Up the stairs to the second floor and not only do the rooms grow uncomfortably small, but the back wall consisted of little more than a thin board covered in paper. Sounds came through from the other side clear as crystal, their fights and conversations so close you could hold them in your hands. I often clamped my palms over my ears and found myself breaking into laughter.

"Again? But it's so hot." Oyuki quickly made for

the small room with the window, and pulled back the fading, pattern-dyed curtain. "Come on over here. There's a nice breeze. Oh, look," she said. "It's flashing again."

"It's cooled off a lot," I said. "Nice breeze."

The view just under the window was blocked by the shade curtain, but across the embankment I could see the buildings lined up, and I could see the face of a woman sitting at the window on the second floor, the shadows of people coming and going, the movement in the street and the town. I could see much further than I had expected. The sky was the color of lead, and it hung heavy over the roofs of the town. There were no stars in the sky, but its underbelly was dyed pink by the neon signs lining the road. It made the hot, steaming night feel even hotter. Oyuki took a cushion, set it on the windowsill, and calmly perched on it to gaze at the sky. Suddenly she reached for my hand and cradled it in hers. "Hey, can I ask you a favor, my darling? When I've paid off my debts. Won't you... won't you take me in?"

"Look at me. How could I do that?"

"You're saying you don't have the right?"

"If I can't feed you, I don't have the right, do I?"

Oyuki said nothing, but started to hum along with the violin song that was playing somewhere off down the street. I tried to lean over and look her in the eye, but she shot to her feet in an effort to avoid my gaze. She wrapped her arms around one of the pillars and leaned her torso outside.

I sat at the tea table and lit a cigarette. "If only I was ten years younger."

"Just how old are you anyway?" She asked.

She had turned to look at me. I raised my eyes to hers and she was smiling, her cheeks dimpled. I relaxed and sighed. "Almost 60."

"Papa? Only 60? You're still kicking." Her eyes flit over my face a few times. "Darling, you're not even 40. Maybe 37?"

"I'm the son of a mistress, so I don't know how old

I am exactly."

"You look young even for 40. Your hair's not graying at all."

"If I was 40, I'dve been born in 1898."

"How old do you think I am?"

"You look 22 or so, but I bet you're closer to 24."

"There you go again—empty compliments. I'm 26."

"Oyuki-chan, you, you said you were a geisha back in Utsunomiya, right?"

"Yes."

"And then you came here? You sure must know a lot about the area."

"Well, I'd been in Tokyo for a while at that point."

"Was there someone with money?"

"Not exactly... I had a patron, but he was sick and passed away. And then..."

"It must have been tough for you. This is a lot different than what a geisha does."

"Not really, besides, I knew what I was doing from

the start. A geisha has to spend so much on things, she'll never get out of debt. Besides... If I'm going to ruin myself anyway, I might as well be able to support myself too."

"You really thought it all out. Did you think through all that on your own?"

"One of the other geisha knew someone that was conducting a business out here. I heard it all from her."

"Regardless, you're really something. Doing all of this on your own—saving up money and all."

"They say my age is perfect for this work. Still, I don't know what the future holds."

She stared deep into my eyes, and I was suddenly uncomfortable again. Could it have been that—there was the feeling, regardless, like something stuck in one of my back teeth. Then it was my turn to look away, turn to the window, and focus my gaze on the sky, or anywhere but on her.

The sky reflected the red neon lights, and was occasionally illuminated by flashes of lightening off in the distance. Suddenly there was a very bright flash, very close by—yet no thunder came. The breeze died off, and the steaming heat of midday threatened to take over the town again.

"Feels like a downpour is coming."

"You know," Oyuki said. "It's *already* been three months since we met in the street."

There was something about this *already* of hers, drawn out and elongated, that carried a vague but pronounced appeal, as if it were reaching back to the distant past and fumbling for something. Had it been a simple, "It's *already* been three months," without any special emphasis then it would have felt like a statement. But this protracted already was not a statement, but a device that reached out and begged for comment, for response. I could feel the answer, Yes, balling up in my throat, but I answered only with my eyes.

Who could hope to count the number of men that sneak down this alley to meet with her each night? And yet, she remembered the day we met? There was something profoundly unbelievable about that to me. She felt a pleasure when reflecting on our meeting. And yet, not even in my dreams, could I have hoped that a girl of this town could hold feelings for an old man like myself; even if she had imagined me 40, I couldn't imagine that she was capable of not only taking a liking to me, but caring deeply for me as well.

As I have already stated many times over, I had various reasons for making the trek out to Oyuki's each night. It was research for *Disappearance*. It was an escape from the radios. It was a reaction to Ginza and Marunouchi, those wretched inner-city towns that drew my scorn. I'm sure there were other reasons as well, but none of them included this woman as a conversation partner. Her house had never been anything but a place to relax for me, and in order to facilitate its use as such, I had told a few lies. They had only been simple ones that came to me nearly at the moment they left my lips, and I had not set out to deceive her. But I had not corrected them since, and with time her misunderstanding of my character had deepened. With words and acts I had hidden my identity, and for that much I suppose I must bear responsibility

Whether it be Tokyo, or overseas, it could easily be said that I know essentially nothing of society other than prostitutes and their world. I would rather not speak of the reason, nor do I suppose I need to. The interested reader may find his interest sated by certain inferior works from my middle years, among them "Early Afternoon," the essay "House for a Mistress," and the story *Unfinished Dream*. All of them are poorly composed and overwrought, and I could not, in good conscience, ask the reader to search them out. Therefore allow me to quote here a passage from *Unfinished Dream*:

He made his visits to the pleasure quarters with such fervor that ten years passed as if they were a day. He knew very well that the quarter was home to darkness and unrighteousness. Had the city come to praise the profligate,

*to call him a just and pious son, he would have refused
their praise even to the extent of selling all of his property.
Indeed, it was his outright indignation at the hypocrisy of
the world and its proper customs that had sent him to the
quarters in the first place, in search of unrighteousness
itself, the darkness that had never affected any other air
than what it was. There was far more joy in discovering a
beautifully patterned cloth cast out among the rags than,
by analogy, finding stains on a wall that had been declared
immaculate. Even in the halls and mansions of the
righteous once can find the droppings of crows and rats. So
too, in the depths of corruption, one may find the blossoms
of human sympathy and perfumed tears. Gather them up.*

Those who have read this passage will no doubt
understand why I felt no revulsion at the dirty ditch and
the women who lived among the mosquitos—why, indeed,
I felt a certain closeness to them.

To facilitate a friendly relationship, and so that

they would not draw away from me in awe upon learning of my person, I thought it best to hide my identity. The last thing I would want is for them to turn me away, or for them to think I was condescending to their lives, as if observing a play. To have an honest relationship with them, I had to lie about who I was.

Once I had actually been told that I was not the sort of person who had any buisness visiting the quarter.

One night, near the bus garage on the "redone street," I was stopped and questioned by a policeman. I genuinely despise announcing myself as a writer and a man of letters, and it stands to reason that I also despise being perceived as such. Being the case, I told him that I was an unemployed vagrant. He quickly took my coat and began to rummage through the pockets. In case of just such an event, I always made a point of carrying my seal and its registration, along with a copy of my family register. Aside from those things I had also been carrying four hundred yen in cash, as I needed to pay the carpenter, gardener, and bookseller for certain services they had rendered me. Upon his discovery of said items the policeman labeled me a landowner, and proceeded to tell me that "a landowner had no business in a place like this. Go on home before you meet with trouble. If you need to be here, come some other time."

I hesitated and he noticed. He quickly took it upon himself to hail me a taxi, open the door, and put me inside. I had the driver continue down the new street and drive a circuit around the entire district before dropping me off and the Fushimi Inari Shrine. Later, I bought a map and studied the layout of the streets so that I might avoid passing a police box in the future.

Just now, when Oyuki mentioned the day we met in that singsong voice of hers, I'd made to answer her but couldn't find the words, and the overwhelming desire to hide my face behind a wall of smoke overtook me. I took out a cigarette. Oyuki, her black, black eyes staring at me, said, "You really look just like him. When I saw you from behind that day I had to catch my breath."

"You don't say. Lots of people look alike from the back," I said, trying to fight the feeling that was overtaking me. Then, "Who? Your old patron? The one who passed away?"

"No... It was when I'd just become a geisha. I thought I'd kill myself if we couldn't be together."

"A rush of blood to the head. I imagine it's happened to everyone."

"And you? You never feel that way do you?"

"Cold as ice, am I? You might be surprised, appearances often deceive, you know. Don't act like you're better than me."

Oyuki just smiled and flashed her dimple. She said nothing. The dimple, deep seated to the right of her pouting lower lip, lent a freshness to her face, like that of a young girl. But it was filled with sadness, it was a dimple she'd forced there by will alone. I quickly tried to change the subject.

"Is your tooth bothering you again?"

"No. They gave me a shot so it's fine now."

Just then, luckily, as our conversation was running out of steam, a customer knocked on the door. Oyuki jumped to her feet and leaned out the window. She pulled aside the blinds and looked down.

"Oh! Mr. Take! Come on up!"

I followed her down the stairs and hid in the bathroom while the customer followed her back up. After I was sure the passage was empty I crept from the house, careful not to make a sound.

Chapter Eight

The expected rain never came. I'd left the room to escape the steaming heat and the clouds of mosquitos, but after a time I realized it was still too early to return. I walked along the embankment and through the alleyways until I came to a small street crossing a little plank bridge. It was lined on both sides by small shops of temple merchants, their businesses further narrowing the passage—already so tight that no vehicle could hope to pass through it. The walk degraded into an endless series of apologies as I brushed passed people coming from the other direction. Just over the little bridge was a small intersection, at which sat a shop selling horsemeat, a stone pillar indicating the entrance to a Zen temple, a torii for the Tamanoi Inari Shrine, and a pay phone. I recalled hearing from Oyuki that the temple held festivals on the second and twentieth of the month, and on those days the streets were filled with stalls and games and throngs of people who rarely ventured back into the alleys. The women working the area called it a shrine for the paupers. I made my way there, as I'd yet to pay my respects.

I've forgotten to mention something critical, so allow me to correct my oversight. Ever since I'd gotten accustomed, both physically and mentally, to making these nightly trips, I'd made a point to take note of the manner of the customers that ply the streets at night, and in doing so have altered the clothes I wear when I come to this town. It is not much trouble. Take the colored dress shirt with its stripes and leave the top button open. Do not wear a necktie. Carry your jacket instead of wearing it. Do not wear a hat. Tussle your hair as if it has never seen a comb. Change into slacks that are worn through at the knee and seat. Don't wear shoes, find a pair of wooden geta that are worn down to the heel. Bring a lot of cigarettes. Et cetera, et cetera. It doesn't require much thought. I simply change out of the clothes I wear in my study, the clothes I wear when I have guests, and I change into my spring-cleaning clothes. As for the geta, I can get them from the servant girl.

As long as you wear old slacks and see to it that your handkerchief is folded in the most haphazard manner you can muster, you can walk from Sunamachi in the south to Senju or Kanamachi in the north without fearing the odd gaze of passing pedestrians. One of the locals may pause in their doorway, perhaps preparing to go shopping, and without a second thought you can walk down their alley. Such slovenly clothes are perhaps more suited to Tokyo's unbearable heat and astonishing cold than any other. As long as you dress the same as the taxi drivers, you can spit on the street and on the train, you can toss your cigarette butts and matchsticks and paper scraps and banana peels wherever you please. You can enter a park, if you so desired, and plop yourself on a bench or sprawl out on the grass and grunt and snore and act how you please. You can abandon yourself to the pulse of a rebuilt city.

My friend Sato Yosai has already written
extensively on the strange summer custom women have
developed of going out on the town in an nightgown-like
piece of cloth. I have nothing to add to his evaluation.

I am not accustomed to wearing geta on my bare
feet, so I have a tendency to slam them against things, trip
over things, step on people's feet, and so forth; I do all I can
to avoid serious injury, and I paid extra attention to my
feet as I pressed throughout the throngs of people on my
way to the back of the Inari Shrine. The stalls continued
all the way to the shrine, to the left of which stood a
reasonably well-sized plot of land that a plant nursery had
taken over, filling it with trees, chrysanthemums, roses,
and potted out-of-season flowerbeds. In a corner stood the
names of people who had donated money to the rebuilding
of the temple. They were inscribed on plaques and lined up
like a fence. Perhaps it had burned down, or, like the
Fushimi Inari Shrine, had been moved from its previous

location.

I purchased a pot of summer flowers, turned down another alley, and made my way back to Taisho Street. I found myself standing just to the right of a police box. I was dressed the same as everyone else that night, and I was holding a pot of flowers, so I thought it would be fine, but, deciding not to risk it, I backed down the alley and turned down another street hemmed in by a liquor shop on one side and a candy store on the other.

The shops that lined half the street, and the alleyways behind them were a maze collectively referred to as District One. Oyuki's house was in District Two, and the embankment that ran through it appeared suddenly at the end of this street in District One, where it bubbled past the entrance to a public bath called Nakajima before winding off through the pitch-dark streets outside the quarter. I thought of the canal, and how it appeared much dirtier than what once surrounded the north quarter. I could not help the sentimental sigh that overcame me when I

remembered that, once, Terajima was just rice fields, the
small river filled with water grasses, small dragonflies
perched delicately on their leaves. It didn't suit a man of
my age. None of the festival carts were out on this street. I
came out by a restaurant under its own flashing neon sign,
which read "Kyushu." Suddenly I could see the lights of the
cars plying the improved road and I could hear the din of
gramophones.

   The pot was getting heavy so I decided to forgo the
main street, turning right at Kyushu instead. The street
was lined on the right by Districts One and Two, and on
the left by District Three, making it not only the busiest
but also the narrowest street. There were kimono shops,
women's shops for western clothing, and western
restaurants. There was a post office box. The night I met
Oyuki, when she ran up under my umbrella—I am pretty
sure that was right around this post office box.

   The remnants of an awkward unsettled feeling
still clung to me in the wake of Oyuki's implied confession,

as if she were joking about her feelings towards me. I realized I knew almost nothing of her background. She'd mentioned being a geisha somewhere, sometime in the past, but she didn't seem to know the various arts a geisha should—so even that was suspect. My first impression, based on very little, was that she had come from a fairly well-off house in Yoshiwara or Suzaki. Perhaps I had been correct.

She did not carry even the hint of an accent, but her face and her clear skin and body make it clear that she's not from Tokyo or its suburbs, which has led me to imagine her the daughter born to parents that moved to Tokyo from somewhere far removed. She was a cheerful girl, and didn't seem to be deeply upset by her current situation. Rather, I could imagine her as bright enough, optimistic enough, to see her current experiences as a way to build a path for herself out of her place in life. As for her relations with men, she listened without hesitation to the lies I issued forth, which made it clear that she was not yet jaded against the world. And if she was able to make me believe that was so, she must have been much more pure hearted and honest than her contemporaries at the cafes in Ginza and Ueno.

I was comparing a showgirl from Ginza to a woman at the window, the latter of which I found more lovable; I felt that we could speak of our feelings more honestly, but, much like the cityscape in the area, upon further reflection I realized she did not think with pride on her superficial beauty, and that there was probably very little chance of thundering disappointment at the gap between her appearance and her person. The street was still lined on both sides by carts and businesses, but here the drunkards did not band together to prowl the streets, and while bloody fights may have broken out in other places, one seldom saw them here. There are other sights to be wary of in Ginza. The middle-aged man, for example, in his perfectly cut foreign suit and distasteful countenance, his hair perfectly styled, his occupation nebulous, swinging his cane as he walks down the street and sings to himself, berating the young women and the children who cross his path. If one only changes into shabby dress and comes out to these outskirts, one is in much less danger, no matter how crowded the streets, than in those back alleys of Ginza, where one must constantly yield way to these distasteful sorts.

The small, lively street with the post office box reaches its height at the kimono shop, after which it continues with rice shops, a department store, fish-sausage shops, and so forth until you come upon a large lumber supply, its boards leaning against the wall. Whenever I get there my legs carry me on without consulting my conscious mind at all, due to the habit it's become. They carry me out to the entrance of an alleyway that stands between the hardware shop and the bicycle parking lot.

Once inside the small alley you quickly come upon the dirtied flags of the Inari Shrine, and the pervasive waves of window shoppers all but disappear. Luckily for me. I sneak down the alleyway, and there are fig trees growing behind the houses and grape vines crawling over the railings, and I look back over my shoulder at the scene, so unlike anything in Tokyo, as I make my way to peer into Oyuki's window.

It looked like a customer was still with her on the second floor, as there were shadows on the curtain. The bottom window hung open. It sounded like the radios out front had finally stopped blaring, so I placed the potted flowers from the festival inside the window and continued on my way to Shirahige Bridge. While I was walking the Keisei buses on their way to Asakusa followed me down the road and passed me. I didn't know where their stops were, so I made no effort to catch one. I kept on walking, and saw all the flickering lanterns at the other end of the bridge.

*   *   *

I've yet to finish *Disappearance*, though I began to write it at the start of summer. Early that evening, when Oyuki said "It's *already* been three months," I realized that it had been even longer since I decided to record the story of Junbei and Mitsuko. When I had last put brush to paper, Junbei had taken Sumiko out of their room to escape the heat. They'd gone to cool off at Shiraghige Bridge, and were discussing the direction they wished to take their relationship. I went to the bridge and leaned against its railings myself.

When I was first toying with the plot of the novel I had intended to make their relationship a rather light matter. However, as the story progressed, that seemed to suit the characters less and less. The heat of the summer grew oppressive along with my confusion, and so I had taken a measure of time off from the project.

And yet, leaning over the railings of the bridge, the echoes of the running river below and the crowds dancing in the park floating over to me, I found myself reflecting on

Oyuki's protracted "*already*," and in doing so decided that Junbei and Mitsuko were not, in the least, unnatural or forced. Their relationship did not seem manipulated by the author (myself) for any effect. Furthermore, if I were to intercede in my original plans and alter the course of their relationship, that alteration itself would stick out.

I took a taxi home from Kaminarimon and, as usual, washed my face, shaved, and lit a stick of incense and placed it in the holder by my inkstone. I reached for my unfinished, abandoned manuscript and began to read it over.

*   *   *

"What's that over there? See it? Is it a factory or something?"

"I think it's a petroleum company. That whole area used to be really pretty—or so I heard. I read it in a book once."

"Want to go for a walk over there? It's not so late yet."

"But there's a police box just over there."

"You're right. Let's go back then. You'd think we were murderers, the way we have to creep around."

"Hey now, don't talk so loud."

Junbei fell silent.

"You don't know who is going to hear you..."

"You're right. But sneaking around and living like this—I've never done it before. It feels... I don't know. I'll never forget it."

"That's why they say to stay away from women... don't they now?"

"Sumi-chan, ever since last night, I feel... I feel like I'm suddenly much younger. I feel like I finally have something to live for. Know what I mean?"

"People are so emotional. Don't get down on yourself."

"I know. But no matter how I may feel, I'm not

young anymore. You'll get rid of me before too long."

"There you go again—even though I keep telling you not to think that way. Just look at me, I'll be 30 soon. Besides, I've already done the things I want to. I'd like to settle down and save some money, you know?"

"You really want to start a little oden shop?"

"I'm going to give the deposit to Teru in the morning. Then you won't have to use your money anymore, right? It'll be just like we talked about last night."

"But then..."

"It'll be fine. You have your savings, so everything else will be fine. I'll take my money and pay everyone off. I'll buy rights and everything. No matter how you look at it, that's the best for everyone."

"Are you sure you can trust Teru? I mean, we're talking about money."

"She's fine. She's rich. She's got the king of Tamanoi as her patron."

"What's that mean?"

"This guy, he owns tons of shops and houses around here. He's around 70 years old too, a really energetic fellow. He came into the cafe sometimes."

"Is that so."

"Anyway, she says that if I'm really going to go for it I might as well go all out. Give up on the little oden shop and take over one of his businesses. Teru and her patron have both said the same thing, they say they'll set me up with a place. But if it came down to it, I wouldn't have anyone to talk things over with. I don't want to run it by myself. If that's how it's going to be I figure it would be easier to just run a little oden shop or a food stall or something."

"So that's why you picked out that plot?"

"Teru is getting money from her mother."

"Very entrepreneurial."

"Well, she's got nerve, but she's no thief..."

Chapter Nine

Tokyo lurched into the middle of September, but the oppressive heat of summer refused to retreat, growing stronger even than August. The window shades caught and flapped in the breeze, slapping against the panes with all the affected air of autumn, but as evening approached the breeze would evaporate, leaving the town stifling in moist heat as if the block was suddenly in Kansai. These nights continued for some time.

Between the composition of my manuscript and my reading, I'd become unexpectedly busied, resulting in three solid days during which I never left my room.

Nothing brought more pleasure to my solitary life than airing out my books in dwindling heat, and the burning of fallen leaves. Those days provide the opportunity to reflect on my shelves of books, to look them over and remember the time, years ago, when I originally found myself entranced by them, and therefore also the opportunity to reflect on the transitory and undulating nature of my feelings and outlook. The burning of the leaves was a brief interlude, during which I could forget my place in the surrounding populace.

I'd finally finished airing out my books that day, so just as soon as I'd had my dinner I slipped into those torn slacks and clunky wooden sandals. By the time I left the house the lanterns at the front gate had already been lit. The lingering heat in the still evenings had not persuaded the sun to stay up any longer, and before anyone had time to notice it had begun to turn out of the sky earlier and earlier.

It had only been three days, but as I passed out the gate I was overcome with the feeling of having neglected a duty, of having been absent from where I had been expected—a feeling that compelled me to hurry on my way. To cut the route shorter I boarded the subway at the Kyobashi station. I had known women from a young age, and it would be no exaggeration to say that I had not felt this flustered over going to see a women in well over 30 years. I took a taxi from Kaminarimon and finally found myself standing, once again, at the entrance to the alleyway. Once again, the standing fox statues. The tattered red banners had all been replaced by clean, white, trailing flags. The same figs, the same grapes, but their greenery had grown almost imperceptibly thinner. No matter how hot the days, no matter how neglected the alley, autumn quietly brought the nights darker and longer.

Oyuki's face was in the same window, but her hair was tied up differently and so, walking slowly and peering intently to ensure I was approaching the correct person I stepped forward into view upon which Oyuki, her patience overflowing, flung the door open and shouted "You!" before quickly slinking back and lowering her voice and continuing, "I was worried. But I suppose that's no matter. I'm glad you came."

I already knew why she was concerned. I sat down on the stoop without removing my sandals.

"You were in the paper, you know. I don't think they got it right, I doubted it the whole time, but still. I was so worried."

"Sorry." Someone had found me, so I lowered my voice as well. "I'm not that stupid. I've been careful."

"But what happened? You seem just fine, but you know if the person I'm expecting doesn't show up I get lonely. I know it's odd."

"But you seem just as busy as ever."

"I found out all this in the heat. It doesn't matter how busy I am."

"Damn though, it really is hot this year," I said, to which Oyuki quickly whispered, "Keep your voice down." She slapped at a mosquito that had landed on my forehead.

The house was filled with more mosquitos than ever. It seemed their needles had grown fatter and sharper. Oyuki produced a tissue from her pocket and wiped the blood from my forehead. "Just look at this." She showed me the stained tissue before crumpling it up.

"When those mosquitos go away the year will be over."

"I know. I think they were still around for the winter festival last year."

For a moment I thought I'd heard her refer to their breeding in the rice paddies, but quickly realized that was a story from another age I'd heard as if in a dream. "You want to go for a walk around here, maybe to Yoshiwara?"

"Sure," she said before turning her head to the gentle chime of a bell in the distance, standing and rushing to the window. "Kane-chan! Over here! What are you standing around for? Get me some iced dumplings and mosquito coils will you? Good child."

She sat at the window, jesting with the passing customers. Occasionally she would speak to me from the space between the Osaka screens. When the man from the ice shop came by she brought something over to me.

"Here. You like iced dumplings, don't you? These are on me tonight."

"You sure remember the little things."

"Of course I do. There's a reason too, so do me a favor and stop these affairs of yours."

"You think I'm running off to someone else's house when I'm not here? Heh."

"That's how men are."

"I'll choke on these things. C'mon, let's get along, at least while I'm eating."

"Whatever," she said with affected scorn, jabbing her spoon into the carefully piled mountain of shaved ice she held.

A customer passed by the window and peaked inside. "Hey there, lady, looks good."

"I'll give you one. Open your mouth."

"I'll pass on the poison. Too young to die tonight."

"You're just another penniless loser, give me a

break."

"What was that? You pond scum!" The man said and walked on. She didn't seem satisfied. "Bastard trash!" She called.

Another passing man burst into laughter.

She spooned some shaved ice into her mouth and left the spoon there, hanging from her lips as she gazed out into the alley and absentmindedly called out, "Hey there, hey there, busy?" To which eventually a man would stop and look over, at which point she'd put the charm on thick and sweetly drawl, "Come on in, I'm not busy. Come on, mister," or, depending on perhaps how the man looked she would turn suddenly businesslike and clip, "Certainly, well, come in for a moment and if you are not satisfied you can just go on your way," to which neither the first or second or subsequent men responded, at which point, without disappointment, unaffectedly, as if reviving an ancient memory, she would return to her melted piled of ice and then fish out a dumpling to chew on, or pull on a stick of tobacco and puff up small plumes of smoke.

I've already attempted to describe Oyuki. She was an energetic woman, and not too depressed over her circumstances. Sitting in the tea room, I could see her through the thin curtains, sitting by the window and fanning away the mosquitos as quietly as she could. Perhaps it was that scene, which had become so familiar to me, that first gave me such an impression. Perhaps my observation had never seen past the superficial, perhaps I'd only ever seen a facet of her true self.

However, there is something to be gained by the assertion of my observation's accuracy. Regardless of the state of her inner self, there was an amicable connection between the outside passersby and Oyuki on the other side of the glass that was harmonious and true. What I mean to say is that if I was mistaken in characterizing her as essentially carefree and untroubled by circumstance, it was no doubt a mistake born of this harmonious, amicable connection. There are masses of people on the other side of the window. The whole world is on the other side of the window. On this side there is only an individual. Between them there was no marked sense of antagonism. And what produced this? Oyuki was still young. She hadn't yet lost her feelings toward the world. When she sat at that window she made herself into something vulgar, all while hiding her other self deep in her chest. The people who passed the window removed and discarded their inhibitions and pretension the moment their feet carried them from the street into the alley.

I plunged myself into this world of rouge and powder at a young age, and I'd yet to awaken and discover a problem with the life I'd lived. There were times when, lost to my emotions for a time, I'd surrender to the request of a girl and bring them into the house and let them hold a broom and clean or whatever it was they were after. But all those ended in failure. The moment the women entered into a relationship and realized that they were not the vulgar, base creatures they had imagined themselves to be, they inevitably made a quick about-face, becoming either a slouch or some type of self-appointed queen.

At some point, Oyuki set her mind on me, on using me as an escape from, or an alternative to, her situation. She wanted to become a slouch or a queen. But whether she would become a queen, whether she'd become a slouch, whether she'd become one of the few satisfied and honestly contented homemakers, whatever she became was not up to me—my past failures an embarrassment of riches—but to those with many, many years of fresh life ahead of them. But if I were to tell her so she would not understand. She'd only seen half of my split personality. It would be a simple matter to learn the contents of Oyuki's undivulged character and to inform her of its imperfections. I could not bear the thought of my hesitation, despite knowing full well the truth of the matter. This was not to protect myself. It was because if Oyuki were to suddenly awaken to the misunderstanding on her own it would, I feared, bring her much disappointment and sorrow.

Oyuki was the very image of the old, nostalgic world made manifest as muse to my exhausted heart. If my manuscript, now placed on my desk for so long, had not drawn Oyuki's gaze in my direction—or at least if I hadn't felt that it had, I would have ripped it to shreds and abandoned it long ago. She was a mysterious encouragement that saw to the completion of this aged, ignored author's final work. A glance at her face fills me with gratitude. Effectively I have taken this girl, so lacking in life experience, and toyed with not only her body, but her very self. I am filled with the desire to apologize for my unforgivable sin, all the while grieving at my inability to do so.

According to what Oyuki said by the window that night, the sad loneliness of my heart seemed to have finally dissipated. To avoid it, all I could do was avoid her face. If only I could have acted then, it might have all ended without necessitating serious pain and desperation for Oyuki. But Oyuki never met with an opportunity to learn of my real name or position in life, and we parted without her ever even asking.

That night, as the moment of our parting grew ever closer, it brought with it a sadness that the truth would never be shared between us, and that when the moment passed it would trail in its wake an irreparable sadness. The deepening night served only to intensify my apprehension.

This feeling, this overwhelming, oppressive, hounding feeling was swept up in the sudden wind that swept into the alley from the main street, twisted here and here, blew into the house through the small window and shook the string hanging from the small curtain bell. The soft chime further agitated my restlessness. It was different than the bells on the sales carts, this bell could only be heard here, in this small and separate world. From the end of summer and into autumn I had never noticed it in the hot, hot nights, but now, the bell softly announced the deepening dark and lengthening nights as if autumn had finally come. Perhaps it was my imagination, but the footsteps outside grew sharper. Somewhere, a woman sneezed.

Oyuki came into the tea room from her perch at the window, drew a flame to her tobacco and, as if recalling from somewhere ancient, said "Can you come earlier than usual tomorrow?"

"How early? In the evening?"

"Earlier. Tomorrow's Tuesday, so there's a checkup. They close at 11, so we can't go to Asakusa. It's fine if you come back around four."

I had thought I could go with her. I had wanted to go and drink to our final farewell, but I didn't want to be seen by reporters or the literati, so I said, "I don't want to go out in public. Do you have something you need to buy or something?"

"I wanted to get a watch. I'll need a winter kimono soon enough too."

"We've been complaining about the heat this whole

time, but I suppose winter's almost on us. How much does one cost? You going to try one on at a shop?"

"Probably 30 yen at least."

"If that's all I've got it here," I said pulling out my wallet. "Go get one made."

"Darling," she said. "Are you serious?"

"Is it awkward? Don't worry about it."

Her eyes filled with unexpected joy, and it filled her face. I gazed at it for a moment, as if to keep from forgetting it, before removing the bills from my wallet and placing them on the tea table.

There came a knock on the door and the voice of the owner. Oyuki had made to say something but she quickly snapped her mouth shut and hid the bills in her belt. I jumped to my feet and passed the boss on my way outside.

I made my way out to the fox statues. The wind was much stronger there, it blew straight in from the street and tousled my hair. Aside from my time in Terajima,

I normally wore a hat on my trips about the city, so as the wind whipped through my hair I quickly threw up a hand to secure my phantom hat. Not finding it, I broke into an awkward grin. The white flags whipped in the wind, their poles bending under the strain alone, with the violent flapping of the curtains from an oden stand. In the abandoned lot the leaves of the figs and grapes jostled in dry, crackling sounds. Out in the main street the widened, clear sky was filled with the Milky Way and the sharp, pointed lights of stars shining across the sky in silence. There was an unspeakable loneliness to it, which combined with the thudding sounds of trains passing behind people's houses, the sirens of police cars, and the sudden, violent winds, all of which further deepened the isolation. On my way home I walked in the direction of the Shirahige Bridge, passed the Sumida Post Office, and ducked into a side street off by a little theater known as the Mukojima, followed it through its twists and turns out past the Rokyoku tower, and came out just behind the Shirahige

Shrine.

At the end of August and the beginning of September the nights would fill with rains that would clear the sky, in which a bright moon would hang, bright enough to light the streets and remind me of the old times. On those nights I'd often walk all the way to Kototoi Hill without a thought, but tonight there was no moon in the sky. The howling wind over the river carried a chill, and as soon as I got to the bus stop on Jizo Hill, I made for the waiting spot and wedged myself between the wall and a Jizo statue to get out of the wind.

Chapter Ten

Four or five days went by, and despite having no plans to visit her again, despite having given her the money for the kimono, I found myself longing to make the trip out to her house by the embankment. I wondered what Oyuki was doing. Despite being very sure she was sitting by the window just as usual, I felt, more than ever, that I simply had to see her face to confirm it. I could go to check on her, just get a look, and if I were careful she'd never know. If I went out there and took a stroll around the town all the radios would be switching off near the time I returned. And so, placing the fault squarely with the radios, I crossed the Sumida River and headed east.

Before entering the alleyway I bought a hat to hide my face and waited for a throng of pedestrians to come. I stepped in among them and peered over at Oyuki's house from the embankment. She was sitting by the window, her hair tied up in a new knot. Everything appeared as usual, except—a window of the same building, to the right of Oyuki's usually darkened one, was lit from within, and the silhouette of an elaborately styled chignon could be seen on the blind. Again and again, another fresh face in the district. I couldn't see very clearly from so far away, but she seemed older than Oyuki, and far less attractive. I rejoined a throng of pedestrians and ducked down a different alleyway.

That night, as had been for so long, the breeze vanished with the sunset and a humid heat over took the city, which I can only assume was the reason that pedestrians came out into the streets in such number you'd think it midsummer and you had to edge sideways by them to get around corners. Sweat running down my brow and out of breath, I rushed for the exit and came to a wide street with no cars. I walked in the opposite direction of the shops and, with every intention to go home, walked to the bus stop on the seventh block and quickly began

mopping my forehead. Perhaps because the stop was only
one or two blocks from the beginning of the line, the city
bus that came, as if rushing there solely for my benefit,
was devoid of passengers. I made to board the bus when
suddenly, and for no apparent reason, I was overcome with
a feeling of regret and pain which caused me to step back
and walk of with no particular destination in mind; after a
few minutes I found myself at the sixth district bus stop,
by the post office box that stood before the liquor shop.
There were five or six people waiting for a bus. I stood
there, filled with regret, and let three or four buses go by
while I gazed off across the poplar-lined street at an empty
lot that stood at the corner to an alleyway. The lot, in the
period that stretched from summer to autumn of that year,
had become once a horse ring, once a space for a man and
his monkey tricks, and finally a show that blared its
phonograph at all hours of the night, hoping to lure in
customers to see their reputed ghosts and ghouls. Now it
stood silent once more, its dim lanterns hanging in the

deepening twilight, their reflections captured on the surface of its puddles

I decided to see Oyuki one last time, tell her I was leaving on extended travels, and break it off. That would be better than just weaseling away and leaving her alone, at least she would not feel like she needed to wait for me. If I could have, I would have preferred to tell her how I really felt. There would be no direction for my walks. Anyone I would have liked to visit has long since passed on. This was not the time for the elderly to slurp at cups of tea and debate the intricacies of medieval arts and their practitioners. In a corner of these labyrinthine streets, and without the intent to do so, I'd discovered what becomes of this sort of life. Therefore, I wished to explain that, even at the chance of becoming a nuisance, I'd have liked to come, however infrequently, to pass some leisurely time. I'd have liked to explain it, though it seemed I was too late. I entered the alleyway once again, and made for Oyuki's house.

"Come on in," she said. Her manner and cadence

suggested she felt as if her expected guest had arrived though, instead of sending me into the tea room as usual she stopped and made to go up the stairs. I looked her over. "Is the boss here or something?"

"Yes, with the landlady..."

"Something new, huh?"

"The lady who cooks came too."

"You don't say. Things sure are lively."

"I'd been alone for a while, so I can't stand all the noise anymore," and then, as if in sudden recollection, "Thank you for the other day."

"Did you find a good one?"

"Yes, they said it would be ready tomorrow. I bought a new belt as well. This thing is so tattered I just had to. I'll go down and show you in a bit."

Oyuki went downstairs and came back with tea. She sat at the window and we made small talk for a little while, but the bosses made no sign of leaving anytime soon. Pretty soon a bell at the inner stairwell rang out—

the sign a familiar customer had arrived.

Unlike when the house had been just Oyuki, it now felt as though I could not stay long. Oyuki seemed preoccupied with the boss as well, so, without ever saying what I'd come to say, and within the space of a half hour, I found myself walking out the door.

Four or five days later, the city had plunged into autumn. The sky seemed somehow changed, and the heavy clouds pushed in by the southerly winds fell low in the sky, dumping their heavy drops across the city before stopping just as quickly. There were times when the rain would continue through the night without pause. The leaves began to fall from the trees in my garden. The bush-clover flowers fell along with them, and the begonias, long bereft of their fruit, painfully lost their color in splotches over their expansive leaves. The garden, thrown into disorder by the wet trees, fallen twigs and leaves, and the remnants of summer crickets and cicadas, left me wishing for breaks in the rain, for the sky to clear just once, and it filled me with grief.

Each year, when I'm overcome with the winds and rains of the season, I'm reminded of a particularly poignant passage from *Dream of the Red Chamber*:

> *The flowers in fall are lonely and fading, the grasses grow yellow.*
> *The moon grows brighter, the nights grow longer.*
> *Autumn, observed from the window, seems never to end.*
> *The winds and rain bring with them a difficult cool dampness.*
> *These rains that rush autumn to us, from where do they come?*
> *From the window, a shock—autumn's dreams of green.*

Furthermore, despite knowing full well that I cannot do it, every year I am struck by the desire, and grief with my inability, to translate it properly.

The seasons changed with the wind and rain, and when the weather cleared, crisp and final, the last September nights were filled with the full moon.

The moon had been lovely for days, but on the night of the full moon all the clouds left the sky.

That was the night I learned that Oyuki was sick and in the hospital. I only heard it from the woman at her window. There was no way for me to learn the specifics.

October brought a chill with it, much earlier than most years. Already, on the night of the full moon there were signs posted near the Tamanoi Inari Shrine saying the time to change out your screens had come. Low prices on good material. The season for open wooden sandals and torn slacks and no-hat walks had passed. It seemed I could enjoy the lights from my room, as my neighbors needed to keep their windows shut, which cut the noise of the radios to a tolerable level.

*   *   *

Perhaps this is where I should stop *Something Strange Across the River*. But if the reader would desire a more traditional ending to the novel I suppose I could oblige by adding that once, half a year later and unexpectedly, I ran into Oyuki in the streets; she was a normal woman then. Furthermore, if I were to elaborate on the meeting to arouse sentiment, I could construct it so that I saw her in a car, or from the window of a passing train, and while we caught each other's gaze we were unable to say the things we wanted to say before the moment had passed. Perhaps we'd catch sight of one another on passing ferries, drifting down the Tone River among the flaming autumn leaves. The odd things people imagine!

Oyuki and I never gave each other our real names or addresses. We had simply grown close in a mosquito-filled house by the embankment that runs through a back town somewhere east of the river. It was a relationship that, once separated, would have been impossible to rekindle, no matter what the desire may have been. While admitting to a certain lighthearted play, if I was to try and speak of the feeling of our parting, despite knowing from the start it would be that way and not expecting or hoping for something else, I could force it and fall into exaggeration, yet if I were to pretend it was nothing would be unjust to the emotion. The ending of Pierre Loti's *Madame Chrysanthème* has already perfectly encapsulated such emotions, and if I were to attempt to conjure them with the ending of *Something Strange Across the River*, it would only draw the scorn of others, those aware of my poor attempts to imitate Pierre Loti.

The time that we spent in the house by the embankment was, by no measure, composed of cheap flattery, it was something I had imagined from a young age. When I was young I'd heard it from an older man, who'd spent his life in the brothels more than anywhere.

"When you find a woman," he said, "a woman you love more than anyone, a woman that makes you feel like you need to rush to her side and confess your deepest desires so as to keep her from being taken by another customer, those are the women that either die of illness or are taken off to some distant land by the most vile men you can imagine." His melancholy musings have proved accurate.

Oyuki was filled with talent and beauty that was without compare anywhere in that quarter. Pearls before swine. But the times have changed and moved on; there was little chance of her death or depression. Little chance that she'd spend her life with an unjust miscreant either.

Once, in that dirtied house, under the dirtied roof paneling, before the onset of a storm, the sky was filled with oppressive, heavy clouds, so low they glowed by the street lights, and Oyuki and I sat at the window on the second floor, sweaty hand in sweaty hand, speaking of mysteries and of nothing. A sudden flash of lightning lit her face. The moment still appears to me as if she were before me. I cannot forget it. I'd lost myself to the games of love when I was near 20, but to think, at this age, I'd find myself overcome. Is it not the height of stupidity to ridicule one's destiny? There are many empty lines left in my manuscript. Perhaps I will allow my brush to fill them, to ease the grief of this night.

> A lingering mosquito
> Stabs my forehead
> Spot of my blood.
> From your pocket
> Produce a tissue, wipe it away.
> Toss it in the corner of the garden.

> The stalks cannot support the weight of the amaranth leaves.
> With night, the fog grows cold.
> Without thought of the evening winds
> The leaves,

Without thought of their approaching deaths,

Their burning embroidery grows brighter,

Even as their stalks bend and curl.

The butterfly grown ill

Totters on broken wings

The flowers bloom in the shadows

Of the dying leaves